This book belongs to

....

....

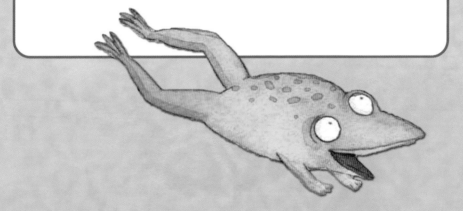

For Isaac (and Froggy)
Also for Andy P.
– L.P.

This edition first published in 2009 by Alligator Books Ltd.
Cupcake is an imprint of Alligator Books Ltd.
Gadd House, Arcadia Avenue, London N3 2JU

Written by Leyland Perree
Illustrated by Joelle Dreidemy

Printed in China 11994

FROG
on the LOG

cupcake

Down in the woods where the river runs through,
By a **creaky** old hut (and a **leaky** canoe),
Stood a marvellous mountain of mossy old logs,
Which happened to house a small family of frogs.

Now those frogs liked to bathe in the stream in the sun,
And roll in the moss (which is good **froggy** fun).
'Til, one day, the river rose up – and the logs
Were washed down the river (along with the frogs).

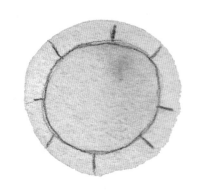

Now frogs are **good** swimmers, I'm happy to say,
So safely they watched their homes drifting away.
As they sat in a row on the bank – **except** one,
Who drifted along on his log, in the sun.

"I **will** not abandon my home!" said the frog.
And he drifted along in the sun, on his log.

An **hour** passed by when the frog saw a dog,
(As he drifted along, in the sun, on his log).
It stood on the bank quietly having a drink,
In the shade of a tree. And it made the frog think:

"Kind dog – I **appear** to need some assistance.
I have drifted downstream a **considerable** distance.

The bank by the hut is the place that I yearn.
To my friends and my family I'd gladly return."

"Small frog," said the dog, "I would carry you **gladly**,
But wood tends to splinter my mouth rather badly.
So ride on my back, if you like," said the dog,
"But you'll **have** to abandon your mossy old log."

"I **will** not abandon my home!" said the frog.
And he drifted along in the sun, on his log.

Another hour passed, as he drifted along,
(Alone, on his log, in the heat of the sun),
When he happened to spy in a nearby bog,
The snout and two eyes of a mud-loving hog.

"Dear hog – I **appear** to need some assistance.
I have drifted downstream a **considerable** distance.
The bank by the hut is the place that I yearn.
To my friends and my family I'd gladly return."

"Small frog – I've been bathing in marvellous muck.
You could cling to my snout, but your log's out of luck.
I'm afraid it would simply slip off," sniffed the hog,
"So you'll have to abandon your mossy old log."

"I **will** not abandon my home!" said the frog.
And he drifted along in the sun, on his log.

The sun now was sizzling high in the sky,
And it beat down upon the frog drifting by,
Laid out on his log as the river's end loomed,
At sharp, jagged rocks (and certain frog doom).

"I wish I'd accepted the help of the dog,
Or hopped on the snout of the mud-loving hog!"

He thought when he saw at the base of those rocks,
The splintered remains of some mossy old logs.

But what was **that** bobbing along in the foam?
A log that was moving **away** from the stone!
There was no time to think (and the little frog knew it).
He took a **deep** breath – then he hopped right onto it.

"How **sad** that I had to abandon my home!"
Said the stubborn old frog, as it **smashed** on the stone.
Then looking about him he saw with surprise,
His new mossy log came complete with two eyes.

"Well, **what** have we **here**?" said the stunned crocodile.
And he grinned at the frog with a wide, **toothy** smile.
"A log-hopping froggy – and I have a hunch,
He hasn't dropped by for a spot of light lunch."

The frog gave a gulp, "This is worse than I feared!"
Thought the frog on the croc and he shed a small tear.
"I'm done for! I've had it! Finito! Ka-put!
I'll never again see the bank by the hut!"

"Now, **now**," said the croc. "Stop crying this instant.
I too have been swept a **considerable** distance.
From **way** past the hut (and the leaky canoe),
I'm heading on back now. Are you coming too?"

So upstream they travelled, the croc and the frog,
And they waved as they passed by the mud-loving hog,
And the dog on the bank in the shade of the tree,
To arrive at the place where the logs used to be.

"Thank you **so kindly** for taking me home!"
Said the frog on the croc, now no longer alone.
And he hopped from the back of the croc to the bank.
The croc waved goodbye – then his **croccy** heart sank.

"Nice frog – I **appear** to need some assistance.
You _see_ I lead rather a **lonely** existence.
My home way upriver was washed away too.
So if it's okay, can I stay here with you?"

And that's how we'll leave them; the **greatest** of friends.
There's no better place for this story to end.
A family of frogs and a crocodile too.
In a **croccy** old hut (and a **croaky** canoe).